Too **Hot** to Handle

Too **Hot** to Handle

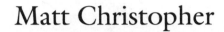

Matt Christopher

Illustrated by Wendy Wassink

Little, Brown and Company

Boston • New York • Toronto • London

FIRST PAPERBACK EDITION

ISBN 0-316-14074-0

LIBRARY OF CONGRESS CATALOG CARD NUMBER 65-10585

10 9 8 7 6 5 4 3

MV-NY

*Published simultaneously in Canada
by Little, Brown & Company (Canada) Limited*

PRINTED IN THE UNITED STATES OF AMERICA

To
Bobby, Sharon
and Gary

Too **Hot** to Handle

1

CRACK! The ball was hit hard. It sped down to third with long hops only inches from the close-cut grass. David didn't move. The ball was coming right at him.

In that second something came over David like a shower of ice-cold water. A ball had never been hit so hard to him before.

He reached down for it. The ball brushed the heel of his glove and shot through his legs. He swung around and saw the white pill rolling fast out to left fielder Marty Cass.

Marty picked it up and pegged it to second, holding the hitter on first.

"Block those drives, Kroft!" yelled catcher Rex Drake angrily. "Fall in front of them if you have to!"

David began to yell to drown out Rex's words. That ball had really been hit. Any third baseman would have had a tough time trying to field it.

The error helped the Gulls. Their next batter socked a clean single over second baseman Ken Lacey's head that sent the runner on first all the way to third.

Brad Lodge got the next two hitters out. The third smashed a line drive to David's left side. David tried hard for it. He was sure he could stop it. It was a high-bouncing ball and wasn't traveling as fast as the one that he had missed.

But he missed it by almost a foot. Shortstop Bonesy Lane couldn't reach it either. The ball bounced out to left field, and the runner on third scored.

The Gulls picked up another run before the Flickers could get them out.

The score was now 4 to 0 in the Gulls' favor.

David went directly to the bench and sat down without looking at anyone. Two grounders that he should have gotten, he thought. Two!

Brad Lodge led off. He flied out on the two-two pitch. Then Ken Lacey put life back into the team as he blistered a pitch for two bases. Chugger Hines socked a single to right, and Ken scored.

The Flickers' bench was once again a bee-hive of excitement. This was the first game of the season. It was the bottom of the third. Up until now the Flickers' wings had really been struggling. But the two straight hits put them back into the game. They were not out of it — not by a long shot.

Jimmy Merrill knocked a sizzling grounder through the Gulls' second baseman's legs, and Chugger went to second. Rex Drake was up. Rex was the Flickers' clean-up hitter.

Chugger began to yell at second to rattle the

pitcher. But his yelling didn't do any good. Rex popped to the first baseman for an easy catch. Two away. He turned and hurled his bat disgustedly to the ground. It bounced a few feet and almost struck little Angie Burns, the mascot.

"Watch that temper, Rex," warned Coach Beach from the bench. "You don't want to be taken out of the game, do you?"

Rex didn't answer. He went to the bench and sat down, squeezing in between David and Ken. Rex was like that. Very touchy.

Marty Cass took a strike and two balls. Then he laced an inside pitch for a clean drive over the third baseman's head, and Chugger came all the way in to home.

Jimmy started for third. Legs Mulligan, the third-base coach, ordered him back to second.

Bonesy was up next with David on deck. Bonesy inherited his nickname from his build. He was so thin his mother had to notch out a hole in his belt to keep his pants from falling.

He took a called strike, then swung at a pitch far below his knees. He fouled the next pitch, then let three balls go by for a full count.

"This is the one, Bonesy," said Coach Beach. "Keep your eye on it."

The pitch came in, and Bonesy swung. A smashing drive to center field! The ball was hit hard. It was half a mile high, and the Gulls' center fielder raced back. Then he stopped, lifted his glove hand, and Bonesy was out.

Two runs, three hits and one error. David dropped his bat and ran out to third. The excited voices of the fans bothered him. The stands were so close to third base that he could hear almost everything the people said.

He wished he could stay at shortstop. He liked it there. But he wasn't good enough. That was why Coach Beach had him exchange positions with Bonesy in the third inning. David had a good arm, but he was short and squat. He was not able to cover as much ground as Bonesy could.

"Think you'll keep up that good Kroft name, David?" a voice said from the stands.

There was humor in the man's voice. There was nothing nasty about it. But the words burned into David's mind.

He knew why that person had said that. Dad had been a great baseball player in his day. Dad had two brothers who were still pretty great. They didn't live here anymore. They had married and moved south. Both were playing baseball with professional teams.

Don was good, too. He was David's older brother. He was sixteen, a junior in high school and just about the best shortstop Penwood High School had ever had. Even Mr. Wooley, the high school athletic coach, said that.

Practically everyone in Penwood who followed baseball knew that there had never been a Kroft who wasn't a good player. A *real* good player.

And that was why the fan had asked David

that question, *"Think you'll keep up that good Kroft name, David?"*

David didn't answer. He didn't even look to see who had spoken. He scooped up his glove, got into position near the bag and waited for the practice throw from first baseman Jimmy Merrill.

Brad bore down on the first hitter. Four pitches and he had the man out of there. Then the Gulls' catcher came to bat. He smashed a hard grounder down to third. It took two hops and was at David before he could blink an eye. The ball bounced up face-high, struck the top of his glove and sailed far over his head.

Another error!

"Come on, Dave!" shouted Rex disgustedly.

The fans yelled. David heard some of them talking to him. He tried to ignore them. He had learned a long time ago that a ballplayer should never listen to what the fans said.

But two errors in one game! How long would Coach Beach stand for that?

David began to chatter, mixing his voice with the rest of the infielders'. It was a good thing Brad was a cool pitcher. It took a lot for Brad to get sore.

The Gulls banged out a hit, but it did no damage. They didn't score.

David led off for the Flickers. He had singled in the second inning. This was his second time at bat.

"Ball!" Inside.

"Ball!" Again it was inside.

"Ball!" Too low.

David stepped back. His heart hammered. The Flickers were trailing 4 to 2. He had to wait out the pitcher.

He stepped back into the box and saw two strikes cross the plate. Full count.

The next pitch came in. It was in there. David swung. *Crack!* A long ball to left field.

Not high enough. It was caught, and David returned to the dugout.

"Tough luck, David," said Coach Beach. "You hit that solid. Legs Mulligan will finish the game at third, David. Warm him up."

"Okay," said David softly.

He went to third to pick up his glove. Some of the fans commented on his hit. He appreciated it, but didn't let on that he did. He and Legs went behind the stands and played catch until the Gulls retired the side.

Legs was built something like Bonesy, except that he seemed to be more legs than anything else. He spat into the pocket of his glove and kept up a steady chatter at third. That was all he did that half inning, just chatter, for not a ball was hit to him.

In the bottom of the fifth Jimmy Merrill walked and finally scored on a single by Bonesy Lane. In the sixth the Gulls picked up another run to make their total 5. Then Ken Lacey knocked another single, his third hit of the game, and Chugger walked. Jimmy flied out, and Rex singled, scoring Ken. That was the best the Flickers could do. They came out on the tail end, 5 to 4.

"Tough game to lose," said Dad as he, Mom, Don and Ann Marie walked out of the ballpark with David. "But it was very exciting."

"Guess it was my fault we lost," said David.

"Because of those errors?" Don laughed. "They were hard-hit apples, mister. I would have had trouble trying to catch those, myself."

I bet, thought David.

"That big mouth," broke in Ann Marie disgustedly.

Mom looked at her. "Who's a big mouth?" she asked, frowning.

"Rex Drake. I heard him say that it looks as if there's one Kroft who won't keep up the good baseball name. Only *he* would say a thing like that."

"Forget it," said Dad. "Just give David a chance. Isn't that right, son?"

David said nothing. He stared at the ground and remembered what that fan had said to him. It was very much the same thing that Rex had said.

2

DAVID knew he might never be as good a ballplayer as Dad used to be. Dad was tall and well-built. He could throw well, hit well and run like a deer. David could throw and hit well, too. But he wasn't fast. He couldn't shift to the right or left as quickly as he should. Nor would his legs carry him as fast as they should. The sprints proved it many times. David would always finish somewhere near the tail end.

Funny how he wasn't born like Don. Don was like Dad. He was fast, too. And shifty. He could play any position on the ball field with ease. Because he was quick and had a terrific arm, Coach Wooley played him at shortstop.

Am I hopeless? thought David. Am I the one who will make people say, "Here is one Kroft who never made it"?

He practiced as hard as he could the next two days. Coach Beach had David alternate at third with Legs Mulligan. David had worried about this before. He had been afraid that Legs might be starting at third. But Legs was a weak hitter, and David could hit. David was sure that that was the only reason why Coach Beach had him start.

Coach Beach knocked grounders straight at David, then to his left side and his right side. David had no trouble catching the big hoppers that came directly at him. And his throws to first baseman Jimmy Merrill were right on target.

But when the coach hit to David's left and right sides, David had trouble. Oh, he caught the high bouncers, all right. His trouble was catching the balls hit hard and close to the

16

ground. These he often missed. And if he fumbled the ball, then picked it up again, his throw to first would be wild.

"Take your time, David! Make your throws good!" advised the coach.

David had heard that advice before. Maybe he just wasn't meant to play baseball. Could you like baseball and still not be meant for it?

Thursday, after supper, David and Bonesy went to see the Penwood Merchants play the Atlas Redbirds. The game was at the Penwood Athletic Field, which had a grandstand behind the backstop and bleachers behind first and third bases. A board fence covered with advertisements surrounded the outfield.

A large crowd attended the game. It had been like this last year. During the first few games of the season the people would come out in droves. Then, as the season wore on, the attendance wore off. It wasn't like the Grasshopper League games. There was always a big crowd watching them.

David enjoyed watching Don play short. In the very first inning Don caught two grounders and whipped them like rifle shots to first. They were easy-to-catch hops, but it was beautiful to watch Don play them. He did it with so little effort.

David paid strict attention to the third basemen of both teams. Since he was playing third now for the Flickers, he wanted to learn all he could about how far away from the bag he should stand, how deep he should play and where to play when a bunt situation came up.

The Redbirds won 6 to 5 on a last-inning home run. Don had socked two hits, both singles, and had about seven or eight assists without an error.

"Too bad we lost that one," David said to Don as they met outside the locker room.

Don shook his dark head. "Give credit when credit's due," he said. "That was a well-hit ball. Just came at the wrong time for us, that's all."

Don was so laid back. Losses didn't seem to bother him at all.

On Friday the Flickers tangled with the Waxwings, who had lost their first game to the Canaries 10 to 2. The Waxwings didn't have any spirit. They were up first, and neither the coaches at the bases nor the players on the bench did any yelling.

"They probably aren't over their loss to the Canaries," observed Rex as he came in to the bench after the Waxwings went down one, two, three. "Look at them. They look half dead."

Then, as if the Waxwings' coach had heard Rex, he began to yell to his team: "Come on! Wake up, boys! Let's hear some noise out there! What happened? Lose your tongues?"

He was batting balls to the infielders. As if his words were a tonic, the infielders began to chatter, and immediately there was life on the field.

"Maybe I should have kept my mouth shut," said Rex.

19

On the mound for the Waxwings was Peter Parker, a southpaw. He was a tall, gangling boy with black hair sticking out from under his baseball cap and hanging over his ears.

Leadoff man Ken Lacey stepped to the plate. He looked very short compared to Lefty Parker. Lefty wound up and delivered a pitch that was a foot over Ken's head. He delivered two more almost in the same place, then hit the plate with his fourth pitch.

Ken walked to first.

"Let him pitch to you," said Coach Beach as Chugger stepped to the plate.

Lefty put the first one over the heart of the plate. Chugger stepped out of the box and looked at the coach.

"Let him do it again," said Coach Beach.

Lefty did it again, and the Waxwings' fans roared. Chugger rubbed dirt on his hands, wiped it off on his pants and stepped back into the box.

Lefty took his time on the mound. He stood

rubbing the ball in his bare hands and looking at Ken on first base.

David, who was coaching first, cupped his hands over his mouth. "Get ready, Ken. If it's a good pitch Chugger has to hit it. And if it's on the ground — go!"

The next two pitches were balls. Then Chugger leaned into the next one and blasted it out to center field. Ken waited halfway between first and second. The fielder caught the ball, and Ken went back to first.

Jimmy Merrill rapped a single over Lefty Parker's head. Lefty missed it, and Ken advanced to second. Rex followed up with another single to left field. Ken rounded third and started for home.

"Run hard! Run hard!" yelled Legs Mulligan, coach at third.

The peg from the Waxwings' left fielder was just as true as could be. It came in as if on a string, and the catcher caught it on the first hop.

"Slide, Ken! Slide!" yelled Marty Cass, who was standing nearby, his bat in hand.

Ken slid. Dust flared up as his feet plowed over the dirt and the plate, just a fraction of a second before the catcher tagged him.

"Safe!" cried the umpire.

Jimmy went to third on the play and Rex to second. Marty Cass took a called strike, then grounded out to short.

Two away.

Bonesy was up. He weaved back and forth with his bat in front of him. No one held a bat like Bonesy. The coach had tried to correct this fault. But with Bonesy it was no fault. He could still bring the bat back and swing it in time.

Lefty delivered two pitches — both balls. Then he sent in a perfect strike. The next was slightly high, but Bonesy swung at it.

A smashing drive to left center field!

Jimmy scored. A short distance behind him came Rex.

David was up next. He swung at the first

pitch and missed. Then he hit a letter-high pitch to center that was caught, and the big rally was over.

The Flickers had scored three runs.

The Waxwings were a quiet, unhappy bunch as they sat in the dugout and watched their hitters go to the plate and be put out. They had been up twice already, and neither time had a ball been hit to David.

The Flickers kept rolling. They scored again in the second and again in the third to bring their total to five. In the fourth the Waxwings knocked out two doubles, one right after the other, and scored twice before the inning was over.

They managed to put another run across in the sixth inning, but that was all. They lost to the Flickers 6 to 3 and walked off the field as silently as they had walked onto it.

David wasn't a bit enthusiastic about his performance today. Not one ball had come to him at third. He had hit a double and had flied out.

In the fifth Coach Beach had taken him out and put in Legs.

Somehow David was glad when the game ended.

An hour later David received a telephone call from Bonesy.

"I found a coin," said Bonesy. "I think it's one you need. Can I bring it over to you?"

"Of course," said David. "Bring it right over, Bonesy."

3

BESIDES playing baseball, David liked to collect coins. He had two folders of them. One held dimes, the other quarters. Grandpa Miller, Mom's father, had given David a good start. Coin collecting was Grandpa's hobby, too.

David looked over his collections while he waited for Bonesy to come. The coins in both folders began with the year 1946. There were three sides in each folder. Each side had slots in which to fit the coins. And under each slot was the year and the number of coins minted that year.

The first side of the dime collection was filled, but the second side still lacked a few. The third side was for dimes that would be minted in future years.

One of the missing dimes was a 1955. That year there were 12.8 million minted, according to the figures under the slot. David had a 1961 dime but not a 1961–D. He had all the other dimes he needed.

He had started to look at the quarter folder when there was a knock on the door. David heard Ann Marie say, "Hello, Bonesy," and then she called to him that Bonesy was here.

"Come in, Bonesy!" said David.

Bonesy came into the room. He was wearing a T-shirt and had combed his hair neatly. He had used a lot of water to comb it, because a few drops were still clinging to it at the ends.

"It's a 1959–D quarter," said Bonesy. "I knew you were looking for quarters with certain dates. That's why I called you."

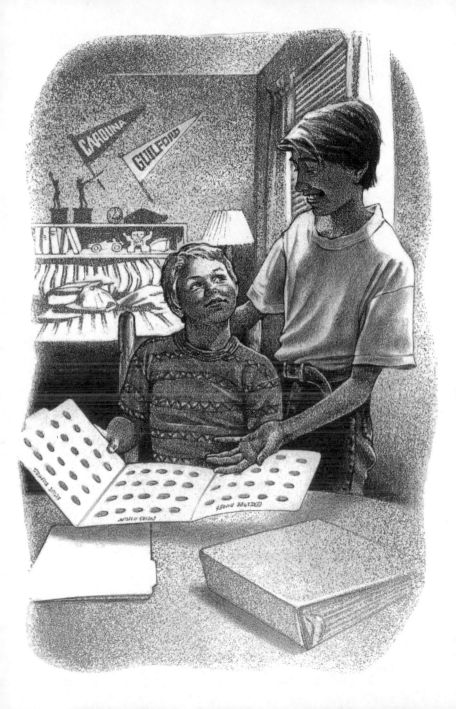

David opened the folder and looked at the slot that was supposed to hold the 1959–D quarter. It was empty.

"Bonesy!" he cried happily. "It's one that I need. Thanks. Thanks a million!"

Bonesy smiled as he handed the coin to David. David looked at the date to make sure Bonesy was right. Bonesy was. Then he pressed the coin into the slot and looked at them all with pride.

"It's almost filled, Bonesy," he said. "All I need is a 1955–D, a 1954–S, a —"

"A 1953–D and a couple more," finished Bonesy, laughing. "And, look — there were only three point two million of the 1955–D's made. Wow! Compared with some of those others, David, that isn't many. Think you'll ever get it?"

David shrugged. "I don't know. I'll just have to keep trying. How much do you want for the quarter?"

"Five bucks."

"What?" cried David. "Five bucks?"

Bonesy chuckled. "Don't get excited. I'll settle for twenty-five cents."

David smiled. "I'll give you thirty cents when I get my allowance."

Bonesy went over and sat on the edge of David's bed. He crossed his arms and sat there awhile, not saying anything. David knew there was something bothering him.

"What's the matter, Bonesy?"

"I've been thinking," said Bonesy. He looked squarely at David. "David, do you want to quit baseball? If you do, I'll quit with you."

David stared. "Quit baseball? Me? What gave you that idea?"

Bonesy looked away again. "Those guys burn me up the way they talk about you. I even told Rex off, but it doesn't do any good."

"Oh," said David. Now he knew what Bonesy was talking about. "I guess it's true what they say, though. I'll never play baseball like my father. Or my two uncles. Guess I just wasn't born to be a good ballplayer."

"But they don't have to say those things," said Bonesy angrily. "You're just as good as I am. You're just as good as many of them are. Look at Legs."

David shook his head. "But his name isn't Kroft."

"That's it," said Bonesy. "That's exactly it. That's why I think it's awful what they say."

"Maybe I should take up tennis," said David.

"But you need money for that," said Bonesy.

"Yeah," replied David. "That's the trouble." He refolded his quarter album, placed it on top of the dime album and put them both back into the drawer of his desk.

"Hit me grounders, will you, Bonesy?" David asked.

"If you say so," said Bonesy. But he didn't seem too happy about it.

David gathered up a bat, glove and baseball and went out to the front yard with Bonesy.

The Kroft house and all the other houses on

the block were set far back from the road, giving each plenty of yard space.

Bonesy stood with his back to the house to hit to David. In this way there would be no danger of breaking a window if he accidentally hit the ball too high.

As David walked toward the edge of the lawn to get into position to field Bonesy's grounders, he spotted Mrs. Finch sitting on the porch across the street. Her full name was Mrs. Gertrude Finch, and there wasn't a person in Penwood who didn't know her. She hardly ever cracked a smile. She hardly ever said nice things to people's faces.

Still, everyone in town liked her. People knew that when she talked back to them in her harsh way she didn't really mean it.

There was one thing about her, though, that David didn't like. Others didn't like it, either. Mrs. Finch belonged to several organizations in town. In every one of them she urged the

31

members to help do away with many of the sports activities, which, she said, were "turning the beautiful town of Penwood into a sports arena."

David couldn't understand why she was so dead set against sports. Mr. Finch wasn't like that at all. As a matter of fact, he attended all the games and enjoyed them. What's more, he bowled.

But that was the way Mrs. Finch was, and nobody could do anything about it. Not even Mr. Finch.

"There's old Crabface," said Bonesy. "Move over. We wouldn't want the ball to go bouncing into her yard if you missed it. We'd never see it again."

A few moments later Mom and Ann Marie left the house. "We'll be back shortly, David," said Mom. "We're going up to see Mrs. White's new baby."

"Where's Dad?" asked David.

"He had to go to a meeting. He shouldn't be gone long, though. Be careful with that baseball, now."

"We will," promised David.

David smiled to himself. Dad belonged to organizations, too. He had helped organize the little league baseball teams and the town team on which Don played. He had helped to organize the Boy Scout troop and had led the fund drive for the new skating rink. He was in nearly every young people's community project that took place in Penwood.

Of course he and Mrs. Finch had arguments about the sports that Dad had helped to bring to Penwood. And the sports' being there was proof that Dad had always won out.

But was Mrs. Finch mad at Dad because he had won? Absolutely not! Mrs. Finch was indeed a most peculiar person. David knew it was just a waste of time for anyone to try to figure her out.

Bonesy kept hitting him grounders. Once in a while Bonesy would hit a hard one. Sometimes David caught it; sometimes he didn't.

And then Bonesy knocked one real hard that David misjudged. The ball bounced up, hit him on the eye, and David fell back onto the lawn. He let out a yell, threw aside his glove and clamped his hands over the eye.

"I'm sorry, David!" Bonesy cried. "I'm sorry!"

David lay on the ground awhile, not moving. He could practically feel the swelling grow under his hand. Boy, did it hurt!

"Look who's coming!" whispered Bonesy. "Old Crabface!"

David started to rise to his feet. He was a little dizzy. He bowed his head and tried to keep from swaying.

"David," came Mrs. Finch's strong voice, "did you get hit with a baseball?"

David nodded. He could hear her snort.

She put an arm around his shoulder. "Come with me. I'll take you to a doctor."

34

"No," he said, and tried to shrug her arm off his shoulder. "I'll be all right."

"Stubborn like your father," she said. "Here. Take your hands away. Let's see that eye."

He let her glimpse it.

"Heavens!" said Mrs. Finch. "You must let a doctor see that, David. Come on. I'll drive you —"

"No. I'm all right now. I'll put some ice on it."

"David!" Mrs. Finch's voice was raised almost to a shout. "If you don't let me take you to a doctor I'll call an ambulance —"

She stopped, for just then a car had turned into the driveway. David looked with his good eye and saw that it was Dad.

Thank goodness! he thought.

4

DAD looked at David's eye.

"Yes, it was hit hard, Mrs. Finch," agreed Dad. "But I'm sure I can take care of it with an ice pack."

Mrs. Finch folded her arms disgustedly. "I'd say you both came out of the same pod," she grunted. "Stubborn as mules, both of you."

Dad chuckled. "A miss now and then does a boy good, Mrs. Finch. The next time David will make sure he has the glove in front of his eye before the ball gets there."

He started toward the house with David.

"Mr. Kroft?"

Dad turned. "Yes, Mrs. Finch?"

"Do all of the lessons you teach your children involve this much pain?"

Dad smiled. "No, Mrs. Finch, don't worry."

Mrs. Finch glared at him a moment. Then she shook her head, laughed and struck her sides with her hands.

"I give up!" she cried. "I give up! Good-bye, and make *sure* you fix up that eye! You hear?"

With that she walked briskly away. David and Bonesy chimed in with Dad's laughter, and the three of them went into the house.

"I can't figure her out," said David.

"Oh, she's all right," said Dad, as he went to the refrigerator and took out an ice tray. "She says she dislikes sports. She wants the clubs she's in to try to stop some of them. She wants more art in Penwood. High-class music, for example. And a children's theater."

Bonesy whistled. "Guess she wants everything high-class!"

"Penwood could still have those things," said

Dad. "All Mrs. Finch has to do is drum up more interest. I just don't like her to step on our toes while she's doing it, that's all."

He put the ice into an ice bag and placed it against David's swollen eye. The eye had already turned colors and was swollen shut.

"Think I'll be able to play baseball next Wednesday, Dad?" asked David anxiously.

"We'll have to wait and see," replied his father.

The day of the Flickers-Bluebirds game came, and David's eye was better. The swelling had gone down, but it was still black and blue.

David played third. The moment he faced the Bluebirds' first hitter, a strange feeling came over him. He got to thinking about his eye. He didn't want to be afraid. He *couldn't* be afraid.

He started up a continuous chatter and pounded his fist into the pocket of his glove. No ball was hit to him that inning. In the next inning and the next he kept up the chatter.

In the fourth a high-bouncing grounder came to him. He caught it, whipped it to first and threw the runner out. He had a put-out that inning, too. A pop fly in foul territory.

He felt better. His chattering had helped him forget about his eye and about being afraid of getting hit again.

The Flickers won the game 6 to 5.

On Friday they tangled with the Canaries. The Canaries had won their first three games. They were still hot as they played the Flickers. Mandy Rubens, their clean-up hitter, smashed out a grand-slam home run. The game ended in the Canaries' favor, 7 to 3.

That evening the sky darkened and thunder rolled. It started to rain, and it rained all night. It rained all day Saturday and Sunday.

The baseball field was drenched. The Monday game between the Flickers and the Waxwings was postponed to July 22 — providing the field would be dry enough to play on then. David was sure that no games would be played that week. It was still raining Monday afternoon.

"I'm getting tired just sitting around and watching television," said Don. "Want to walk to the library with me, David?"

"Sure," said David.

They put on their boots and raincoats and went out into the rain. The Penwood Public Library was on another street, just beyond a narrow wooden footbridge that crossed Indian Creek.

For a while they stood on the bridge and watched the water flowing underneath. It looked wild and dangerous. Up the creek David could see the high falls in the distance. Never had he seen so much water come over the falls before.

The sight made him tremble. "Let's go, Don," he said.

They continued on to the library. Don picked up two adventure novels and two sports novels.

41

David selected a horse story and two books on baseball. They put the books underneath their slickers and started back for home.

Partway over the bridge, Don suddenly stopped.

"David!" he said. "This bridge is moving!"

David noticed it, too. "Let's run for it!" he shouted.

They started to run. They were nearly across when the bridge broke loose from its holdings in front of them. David felt the wooden plankings give way under his feet and the cold water rush across his legs as he went down with the bridge.

He yelled with all the strength he had in his lungs. At the same time he let go of the books and grabbed hold of the railing. In the next second the bridge tore loose at the other end and shot downstream. David turned and saw Don clutching the railing desperately, too.

Don was on one knee. The railing from the other side was lying across his leg.

43

5

THE bridge was like a raft carrying the two boys down the stream. It bobbed and see-sawed with the swiftly flowing water.

"David!" shouted Don. "Duck your head! We're coming to a bridge!"

David had seen the bridge ahead of them. There were only a few feet of space between it and the flooding stream.

He ducked his head. This was going to be close. Real close!

Seconds later they were under it. There were only inches between the top of the railing and the bridge, but they passed safely through.

David heard shouts behind him and looked back. A couple of cars had stopped on the street. People were jumping out of them, pointing at the boys. Yelling.

The brothers had to pass under another bridge. Fear gripped David again. But they passed under this one safely, too.

Gradually the stream widened. The water became less bumpy. It didn't splash over the bridge anymore. The ride was easier. Less than a hundred yards away was the lake.

David saw Don lift the railing off his leg and heave it back. Then he saw Don rub his leg, saw the pain on Don's face.

"You hurt bad, Don?" David asked worriedly.

"I don't know," said Don. "That railing hit me pretty hard."

David raised himself with difficulty to his feet. When he stood at the railing, he could see that Don was favoring his hurt leg.

A few minutes later they were out on the lake.

"Well," smiled Don, "that was quite a ride. We'll never forget this one, will we, David?"

David grinned with relief. "Wow! I guess not!"

They heard the sound of a motorboat. In a moment they saw it coming across the waters from Regent's Boat Landing.

The boat came up close. There were two men in it. The boys knew them both. The one with a straw hat was Mr. Regent himself. The other was Mr. Thomas, a man who worked at the landing.

They pulled up alongside the bridge. Mr. Thomas stood up and held on to the bridge railing while the boys got into the boat.

David hopped in easily. But Don had trouble. He couldn't walk on his hurt leg. He got down on his knees and crawled backward into the boat. David saw Don wince from the pain, but Don didn't utter a peep.

"You boys had quite an experience," said Mr. Regent, as he revved up the motor and headed

47

the boat back toward the landing. "Lucky you both weren't thrown off. The waters are mighty dangerous up at the other end."

"You can say that again," replied Don.

"We lost our books," said David.

"Books?" echoed Mr. Regent.

"Yes. We were just coming back from the library. I had three books and Don had four. We lost them all."

"Don't worry about them," said Mr. Regent. "Books can be replaced. Your lives can't."

When they arrived at the landing, Mr. Regent and Mr. Thomas got on either side of Don and helped him out of the boat. An ambulance was standing by, waiting for him. Don was laid on a stretcher and put into the ambulance.

"Can I go with him?" David asked the driver.

"You sure can," said the driver.

"Will you please call my mother and tell her about this, Mr. Regent?" said Don. "And tell her not to worry."

48

"Of course, my boy." Mr. Regent smiled.

At the hospital, X rays were taken of Don's leg. They showed that the bone just above the ankle was fractured.

Mom, Dad and Ann Marie were there. Mom had called Dad immediately at work after she had received the message from Mr. Regent about Don.

"We'll have to put a cast on that leg," said Dr. Stevens, a small, chunky man with glasses. "And keep Don here for at least a week. That isn't bad at all, you know. Those boys were very lucky."

"Will he — will he be able to play baseball anymore this year?" David asked worriedly.

The doctor smiled at him. "I'm afraid not, David. I guess you'll be the only Kroft we'll be watching the rest of this year. Don will have to sit it out."

6

WHEN David woke up the next morning the sun was shining through the window. He leaped out of bed and pulled aside the curtains. Below him the front lawn was green as a freshly scrubbed rug. A breeze was teasing the leaves of the big trees that lined the street. How good it was to see the sun again!

He dressed quickly, went to the bathroom and washed. Then he hurried downstairs. He had reached the bottom when he remembered.

Don is in the hospital. His leg is fractured. He can't play ball anymore this year.

Mom and Ann Marie were up. Ann Marie

was practicing the piano in the living room. Mom was at the telephone. She was telling someone about the bridge accident and about Don's being in the hospital.

That evening the paper had several pictures concerning the accident. One showed the place from which the bridge had been carried away. Another was of the bridge floating out in the lake. There were also pictures of David and Don and a long article about their hazardous journey down Indian Creek.

Penwood wasn't the only town struck by the flood. Other small towns in the valley had been struck, too. Some much worse.

David worried about the library books. He spoke to Mom about them. She suggested that he telephone the library and tell them he would pay for the books.

"Don't worry about it, David," said Ms. Benson, the librarian. "I'm just grateful you boys saved yourselves."

"Thank you, Ms. Benson," replied David. But

51

someday he hoped to repay the library for those books. He knew they were expensive and that the library was allowed only so much money each year for books.

By Thursday the baseball diamond was dry enough to play on. The Flickers met the Gulls. David didn't start. Coach Beach had Legs Mulligan start at third base and David coach third when the Flickers were up at bat.

Legs didn't do badly. He handled two grounders and a high pop fly without an error. In the third inning a hitter dragged a bunt down the third-base line, catching Legs off guard. Legs charged the ball, picked it up and heaved it to first. He ignored the shouts of "Hold it, Legs! Hold it!" that his teammates yelled at him, for the runner was almost on first before Legs had the ball.

But Legs threw anyway, and the ball sailed far over first baseman Jimmy Merrill's head. The runner took another base. A hit scored him.

In the top of the fifth David pinch-hit for Legs. Bonesy was on first. Dick Baron, the Gulls' pitcher, had walked him. Dick's first pitch to David was wild, and Bonesy went to second.

With one ball and no strikes on him, David let the next pitch go by. Ball two.

The Gulls' catcher carried the ball back to Dick Baron, said something to him and walked back. The next pitch Dick threw in was a strike. He followed it up with another one. David saw it coming belt-high. He swung hard. *Crack!*

The ball arched over the shortstop's head for a clean hit, and Bonesy scored. When the center fielder pegged the ball in to home, Herm Simmons, coaching first, yelled, "Run to second, David! Run!"

David raced to second. He heard Herm yell, "Hit the dirt!"

He hit the dirt. The second baseman caught the peg from his catcher and put it on David. But David had slid under him.

"Safe!" cried the umpire.

David rose. He brushed the dirt off his pants and stood with one foot on the bag, panting for breath.

Nobody knocked him in. The Flickers were leading 3 to 2.

Bottom of the fifth. The first batter for the Gulls drove a hard grounder to David's left side. It was one of those a faster player would have caught. David didn't. The ball went for a base hit.

"Play in, David!" yelled Rex Drake. "Play in!"

That's right, David thought. This could be a bunt. I should have thought of that myself.

He stepped forward until he was on the grass and ahead of the third-base bag by about three feet.

The pitch. It *was* a bunt. The batter laid it down neatly toward third.

David charged forward. He scooped up the ball. Fumbled it! He picked it up again, pegged hard to first.

Safe by a half a step!

The Gulls' fans roared. Whistles shrilled.

David struck the pocket of his glove angrily with his fist. An error the first thing.

"You'll never make a good Kroft player playing like that, David!" yelled a fan in the bleachers.

The words drummed in David's mind. He started to chatter then. It was the only way he could ignore the ugly things the fans were saying.

Brad Lodge bore down on the next hitter. With two balls and two strikes on him, the batter hit a hot grounder to short. Bonesy fielded it and whipped it to Ken. Ken stepped on second and pegged the ball to first.

A double play!

"Thataboy, Bonesy!" David yelled. "Nice play!" That double play had saved him from being the cause of a possible run.

The Gulls' next hitter hit a high pop fly between third and home. David hollered for it. The ball looked like a dot as it soared toward the blue sky. David watched it closely as it started downward. He was sure he was directly under it.

Then he saw that it was falling behind him. Quickly he stepped back, reached up his glove. Caught it!

The Flickers' fans cheered. Some of the Gulls' fans laughed. "Almost lost it, David!" they said.

The Flickers picked up another run at their last turn at bat. The Gulls couldn't get a man past third, and the ball game ended with the Flickers winning, 4 to 2.

Dad, Mom, David and Ann Marie visited Don at the hospital that evening. Don was in a happy mood. His leg was in a cast, but he did not seem discouraged at all.

David looked at him wonderingly. Don knew he was not able to play baseball anymore this year. How could he be so cheerful?

And Don was a good player. He was the best. I'd be sick all over if it were me, David thought.

After Dad, Mom and Ann Marie spoke to

Don awhile, Don turned to David with a pleasant grin on his face.

"Well, brother, how did you make out today?"

"We won," said David. "Four to two."

"Fine. Get any ground balls in that hot corner?"

David shrugged. "Well, I only played the last two innings. I caught a pop fly. And I made an error."

"It was a drag bunt," explained Dad. "David had to run in fast for it. He fumbled the ball."

"He threw to first and nearly got the runner, too," added Ann Marie.

Don smiled. "Drag bunts are tough. All kinds of bunts are tough to field. That's why I play short." He laughed and punched David playfully on the chest. "Keep working hard, kid. You'll have to take over now, you know. I can't play anymore. At least not anymore this year. It's up to you to keep the name of Kroft going."

David stared at Don. His heart began to pound, and he took his eyes away from Don's.

He felt Dad's hand on his shoulder and heard him chuckle.

"Don't worry about it, David. No one is going to really care how well you play. When you're on the ball field do the best you can. That's all anyone expects of you. Isn't that right, Don?"

"Right," said Don.

But that wasn't so. And David knew it.

He *had* to play better. Much better than he was playing now.

7

RIGHT after lunch on Saturday afternoon, David and Bonesy walked to the library. They went by where the old wooden bridge had been. No start had been made yet in replacing it. There was a sign: DANGER.

The boys walked down a path that ran parallel with the creek. They crossed the bridge at the street. It was the only way now to reach the library from where David lived.

David talked to Ms. Benson. He said he'd like to take a few books to Don in the hospital. Was it okay?

It was indeed okay, she said.

"Don and I . . . we'll pay for those books we lost," said David.

Ms. Benson smiled. "I told you not to worry, David. The library board knows about it. They're going to talk with the city officials to see if they can use some special funds to replace the books. How is Don?"

"He's coming along fine," said David.

Someone stepped up to the desk beside David. "Why, David Kroft! How are you? And how is your eye?"

David turned. There stood Mrs. Gertrude Finch, smiling at him as if she had succeeded in getting rid of all the sports activities in Penwood.

"I'm fine, thanks," said David. "And so's my eye."

Mrs. Finch looked at the eye closely. "Just a little coloring left. But it's pretty. By the way, what are you two boys doing this afternoon?"

David looked at her. "Nothing," he said.

"We have a ball game at four o'clock," reminded Bonesy. "That postponed game with the Waxwings."

"Well, I have a job to be done at our cottage," said Mrs. Finch. "Mr. Finch is working and can't be there. I'm going over now to clean inside the cottage. But I need help to clean up the yard. I could use two volunteers. They'll get paid, of course."

David looked at Bonesy, and Bonesy looked at David. Then David looked at Mrs. Finch.

"Can you get us back in time for the game?"

"Of course."

"We'll go," he said.

"Fine!" Her eyes blinked happily. "Better call your mothers. Tell them where you're going."

David told Ms. Benson he'd pick up the books later. Then the boys called up their mothers. In no time they were piled into Mrs. Finch's car, driving out of the parking lot and up the street.

Mrs. Finch's cottage was about six miles from Penwood. To get to it Mrs. Finch had to cut off from the main highway onto a narrow dirt road. The recent rain had left it filled with ruts. The ditches on either side were deep and dangerous. The hill was steep, and Mrs. Finch was forced to drive very slowly and carefully.

At last they reached the cottage. Immediately David and Bonesy saw what Mrs. Finch had meant. The yard was covered with dried leaves and broken, dried-up twigs. The lawn needed cutting. Indeed, the place needed a thorough cleaning-up.

"There you are," said Mrs. Finch. "Your work is cut out for you. Put all the leaves and twigs into that big rubbish can there. When you're ready for the lawn mower, it's in the garage."

The boys started working. Slowly but surely the yard began to look a lot better.

Some time later Mrs. Finch came out of the cottage. She had changed into a pair of jeans and had put a white painter's cap on her head.

She certainly did not look like the Mrs. Finch who belonged to social clubs and wanted Penwood to have less sports and more art and music.

"Doing fine, boys," she said. "Look, I have to get back to Penwood for a few minutes. I'm all out of kerosene. And I can't heat water without kerosene. The kitchen floor needs washing terribly. I'll be back before you can say Peter Piper picked a peck of pickled peppers."

She got into her car and drove off.

"I hope she'll be back," muttered Bonesy quietly.

"You don't think she's going to leave us here, do you?" said David.

They finished cleaning up the yard. They took the mower out of the garage and started to cut the grass. It wasn't a power mower. The grass was nearly six inches high, and it took both boys to push the mower through it.

Once they paused and wiped their brows

on their shirtsleeves. Trees provided beautiful shade over most of the lawn, but the afternoon was scorching hot.

"She should be back by now," said David.

"Wonder what time it is," said Bonesy.

Neither one had a watch. David walked to the cottage. He opened the door and looked inside. A clock was on the wall above the kitchen table.

Five minutes after three!

He closed the door and ran back to Bonesy.

"Bonesy! It's five after three!"

"Geez Louise!" cried Bonesy. "Isn't she ever coming back?"

They kept mowing the lawn, worrying more every minute. At last they finished mowing, and David went to see what time it was now.

Twenty minutes of four.

"Something's happened," said David. "Maybe she got into an accident or something."

Bonesy's face was red. "Boy! What are we going to tell Coach Beach?"

"We'll have to tell him the truth. What else?"

They sat on the grass with their arms crossed over their knees. They were mad, disgusted and afraid. Mad and disgusted with Mrs. Finch, and afraid of what the coach was going to say.

This is the last time I'll ever do this, thought David angrily. The last time!

The next time David looked at the clock it was ten minutes of five.

"Let's walk home," said Bonesy. "Those train tracks will take us straight to Penwood."

There were railroad tracks along the side of the lake. A freight train went over it once a day.

Bonesy rose and brushed the grass off his pants. He opened the gate and walked down to the tracks.

David watched him a moment. Then he rose and followed Bonesy. Bonesy was walking rapidly, his long legs stepping on every other tie.

David followed him awhile, but it bothered him. They couldn't just walk away like this. They just couldn't.

He stopped walking. "Bonesy!" he yelled.

Bonesy paused and looked around. "Oh, come on!" he said.

"We can't, Bonesy," said David. "She might come any minute. If she doesn't see us she'll get worried. Let's go back. We'll walk up the hill. Maybe we'll meet her coming down."

Bonesy looked at him a moment. David thought that Bonesy would put up an argument, but Bonesy didn't.

"Maybe you're right," he said. "But, boy, I'll never do this again!"

They retraced their steps to the cottage. David saw that they had forgotten to put the lawn mower back into the garage. They did, then started walking up the hill.

They had covered nearly half a mile when David stopped and stared.

"Bonesy," he said, pointing straight ahead. "Look!"

Coming slowly down the hill toward them was Mrs. Finch's car.

8

WHEN Mrs. Finch reached the boys the first thing she said was, "I'm so sorry, boys! I'm so sorry!"

"What happened, Mrs. Finch?" asked David, wide-eyed.

Her hands and clothes were smeared with dirt.

"Please get in," she said. "I'll tell you."

David and Bonesy piled into the car. Mrs. Finch released the brake and continued slowly down the hill. On the floor near the back-seat was a five-gallon metal container. The boys could hear the kerosene sloshing inside it as the car waddled down the rut-filled road.

"I had a flat tire," said Mrs. Finch.

No wonder Mrs. Finch's hands and clothes were so dirty, thought David.

"Did you change the tire yourself, Mrs. Finch?"

"I tried. But I could barely lift the tire, let alone jack up the car. So I walked a way on the highway and flagged down a car. You'd be surprised how many drivers there are who are afraid to pick up a stranger!"

David listened with interest. "Did you walk all the way to Penwood?"

"No, thank goodness. Some kind soul finally picked me up. I got Jim Foxx, the young man who works at the gas station, to come and change the tire for me. But business was so heavy then that he couldn't leave immediately. Boys, believe me. I'm sorry. And that wasn't all."

David and Bonesy stared at her.

"After Jim changed the tire I drove to Penwood. I purchased the kerosene and immediately headed back for the cottage. I guess I must have pushed the gas pedal harder than the law allowed. Anyway, that's what the trooper told me when he stopped me and handed me a slip of blue paper."

Bonesy's brows arched. "Were you stopped for speeding?" he murmured.

Mrs. Finch nodded. "That I was, Bonesy, my boy."

They reached the cottage, and Mrs. Finch drove the car into the garage.

"We're sorry about that, Mrs. Finch," said David humbly.

"So am I," said Mrs. Finch. "But I'm even sorrier than that. I really wanted to get you boys to your ball game. Whatever things you've thought of me before will be worse now. I wouldn't blame you if you hanged me in effigy."

"We'd never do that, Mrs. Finch," said David. "You couldn't help what happened."

Mrs. Finch turned off the ignition and looked

at David and Bonesy. Then she blinked, turned and got out of the car.

"Come on, boys," she said. "I'll cook some supper for us, and then we'll go home. By now that ball game is over, anyway. I just hope your team won."

When she saw how cleaned and neat the yard was, her face lit up. "My! That looks just beautiful!" she said.

She washed, put on her other clothes, then cooked supper. The boys ate hungrily.

When they got back to Penwood, Mrs. Finch drove the boys to the ballpark. It was almost empty except for some players and Coach Beach, who were putting the baseball equipment away. Mrs. Finch gave each of the boys ten dollars. They thanked her, and David said happily, "Maybe I can buy some of those coins I still need."

Mrs. Finch's eyes widened with surprise. "Do you collect coins, David?" she asked.

David nodded. "Good-bye, Mrs. Finch."

"Good-bye, Mrs. Finch," said Bonesy.

"Good-bye, boys," said Mrs. Finch, and then she drove off.

The boys walked into the ball park and up to Coach Beach. They stood nervously behind him as he pushed the last of the baseball equipment into a large canvas bag.

"Coach," said David. He swallowed; his heart was thumping like a hammer.

Coach Beach turned. His eyes narrowed when he saw who it was. "Well," he said. "Welcome back." He looked angry and disgusted.

David wet his lips. "We want to apologize, Coach. We couldn't help it. We —"

Then Coach Beach's face broke into a smile, and he laughed.

"Never mind, boys. I know all about it. Mrs. Finch explained it all, so you have nothing to apologize for."

David's and Bonesy's faces dropped in amazement. "Mrs. Finch told you what happened?"

Coach Beach nodded. "She did. Told me

about the flat tire and her trouble in catching a ride. So don't worry. I'm not going to bench you for not showing up."

"She was stopped for speeding, too," said Bonesy.

The smile on Coach Beach's face disappeared. "She was?"

The boys nodded. "She got caught speeding when she went back to the cottage with the kerosene," explained David. "Guess she wanted to get us back here in time so that we wouldn't miss all of the game."

"Poor Mrs. Finch." The coach shook his head regretfully. "She really had tough luck today, didn't she?"

"Guess it was partly our fault," said Bonesy. "She wouldn't have been stopped for speeding if it wasn't for us."

Coach Beach grinned. "You're right, Bonesy. That part was your fault."

"Who won, Coach?" asked David.

"The Waxwings. Eight to six. Maybe you had something to do about that, too. I don't know. Anyway, make sure both of you are at the next game."

"We sure will," said David, and then he looked at Bonesy.

It had been a rough day all around.

9

DAVID asked Dad to knock him grounders in the front yard. Dad reminded him of the black eye he had received from a bad bounce and suggested that they go to the ballpark.

David called Bonesy, and Bonesy went with them. Dad hit grounders to David's left side and his right side. David fielded the big hops easily when the ball wasn't too far either way. Dad hit other grounders right past him, grounders that would have been caught by a faster player.

David struck the pocket of his glove angrily when he couldn't catch those.

"Never mind," said Dad. "They would be tough ones for anybody to catch."

But David had seen third basemen spear grounders and line drives that were hit hard on either side of them. It was plays like those that made a good third baseman.

He remembered what Don had said in the hospital: It's up to you now to keep the Kroft name going.

Somehow he wished that Don had never said that.

It sprinkled a little Monday morning. The Flickers went to the ballpark early in the afternoon. The rain had settled the dust around the base paths and the pitcher's mound. For an hour Rex Drake had the infielders practice on grounders and the outfielders shagging flies. During the next hour they held batting practice.

Rex was captain and handled the team when Coach Beach was working and couldn't be there.

Later, before the six o'clock game started, there would be men here who would rake the infield and line the base paths and the batter's box with white lime.

The Flickers practiced again Tuesday morning, and David worked as hard as he could at third. He alternated with Legs Mulligan. Legs didn't seem to try half so hard as David, yet he fielded the ball more easily and made the catches look simpler.

David didn't know whether Rex said anything about him to Coach Beach. But when the Flickers played the Canaries the next evening, David didn't start.

The Canaries had not lost a game. They had won seven straight. The Flickers had won three and lost three. It was in the heart of every boy on the Flickers' team to beat the Canaries today.

The crowd was larger than usual. David saw

that there were more Canaries' fans there than Flickers'. And they were sitting on the third-base coaching box side.

The Flickers were up first. They got off to a poor start as leadoff man Ken Lacey struck out. Two fly balls to the outfield ended the Flickers' half-inning.

Brad Lodge threw in the warm-up pitches to Rex, but when he faced the first Canaries' batter he had trouble. He gave the man a free ticket to first on four pitched balls. The next batter bunted to Legs at third. Legs tried to throw the man out at second, but the ball reached there too late.

Brad was nervous now. He rubbed his forehead with the sleeves of his jersey and kept jerking his shoulders. He toed the rubber, delivered, and the batter turned his bat toward the ball as if to bunt. The pitch was low.

"Ball!" said the umpire.

The batter went into the same motion several more times, and Brad didn't put one over the plate. He gave the man a free ticket, too, and the bases were loaded.

Rex called time and went out to talk to Brad. Legs and Jimmy Merrill walked over to Brad, too. They talked with him awhile, then returned to their positions.

Whatever they said didn't do any good. The first pitch Brad put in there was hit for a line drive over short. Two men came in, and the hitter stopped on second for a clean double.

The Canaries' fans went wild. It looked surely as if the yellow birds were heading for their eighth straight win.

Then Brad struck out the next hitter, and the next two flied out.

Rex led off in the second. He uncorked a double, went to third on Marty Cass's hit to right field, then scored on Bonesy's single.

Legs grounded out to second, Marty was caught trying to steal third, and Windy Hill swung at a third pitch that was far too high, ending the half-inning.

The Canaries kept rolling. They got two hits at their turn at bat and racked up one run. Now it was 3 to 1 in the Canaries' favor.

David heard the Canaries' fans yelling cheerfully. Even the players were laughing and joking away in the field, confident that this was just another game. That they would put this one in their pocket, too.

Brad Lodge, leading off in the top of the third, gave the Canaries more to cheer about as he went down swinging. Then Ken changed the picture. He belted out a single and went to second when the shortstop missed Chugger Hines's smashing grounder.

The coach gave Jimmy Merrill the bunt signal. It would be better to have men on second and third, in scoring position, than to take the chance of having Jimmy hit into a double play.

Jimmy missed the first pitch. He fouled the second and struck the plate disgustedly with the tip of his bat. Now he had to swing.

Rocky Stone, the tall right-hander for the

81

Canaries, delivered a pitch just level with Jimmy's knees. Jimmy swung. Out!

Rex was up. He had doubled his first time up. Could he repeat?

Apparently Rocky Stone didn't want him to. He walked Rex to load the bases.

Now it was the Flickers' fans' chance to cheer. And they did.

"Come on, Marty!" they yelled. "Drive it out of the lot! Blast it over the fence!"

Rocky took his time. He removed his cap and wiped his brow with his sleeve. Then he looked for the signal from his catcher. He nodded, stepped on the rubber, made his stretch and delivered.

"Strike!"

The Canaries' fans shouted happily. "Thataway, Rocky! He's your man now!"

Marty waited for the next pitch. He held his bat high and his legs close together. The pitch came in. He swung.

"Strike two!"

"He's all yours, now, Rocky boy!" yelled the Canaries' catcher.

Marty almost swung at the next one. It was wide.

"Ball!" said the umpire.

Rocky still took his time. He picked up the rosin bag, rubbed his fingers on it a moment, then dropped it. He toed the rubber, stretched and delivered the pitch. Like a white bullet the ball sped toward the plate. Marty swung.

Crack! A smashing drive over short! Ken scored. Not far behind him came Chugger. The shortstop caught the throw in from the center fielder and made a beautiful peg to the catcher. Rex held up at second.

The Flickers' bench went wild.

Bonesy struck out. But the Flickers were strongly back in the game. They had tied it up, 3 and 3.

Mandy Rubens, the Canaries' slugging out-fielder, broke the tie with a blast over the left-field fence with the bases empty.

The Flickers came to bat in the top of the fourth, trailing by the score of 4 to 3. It was a close game so far. The Canaries were a different bunch in the field now. They were not laughing and joking. They were serious. They had begun to realize that this was a game they could lose.

David started to run toward the third-base coaching box when he heard Coach Beach yell at him.

"David, bat for Legs! Let's see you get a hit, kid! Start a rally."

David looked at the coach. Something cold gripped him. He didn't move for a moment. He almost wished that Coach Beach wouldn't ask him to go into the game. Legs was doing all right. Why not let him stay in?

David walked to the bats lined up on the ground. He picked up his favorite one, put on a helmet and stepped to the plate.

He was not only nervous as he waited for Rocky Stone to throw. He was frightened, too.

10

"STRIKE!" The ball was over the heart of the plate. David pursed his lips. He felt as if someone had kept him from swinging the bat.

Rocky threw a couple outside, then put another one over the plate. David corked it. It was a long high fly to left field.

He dropped the bat and raced for first. Just as he made the turn, the first-base coach, Herm Simmons, yelled for him to stop. The left fielder had caught the ball.

Steve Pierce pinch-hit for Windy Hill. He did better than David. He singled on the second pitch and went to second when the center fielder missed Brad Lodge's fly. Chugger got a single that inning, too, but no Flicker went past third base.

David caught a few warm-up grounders from Jimmy Merrill before the first Canaries' batter stepped to the plate. The batter hit the first pitch down the third-base line, and David leaped after it. The ball struck the top of his glove, shot up into the air and dropped behind him. David picked it up and pulled his arm back to throw.

"Hold it, Dave!" yelled Bonesy. "Hold it!"

Angry with himself, David shook his head and tossed the ball to Brad. He ran back to his position, then realized that a bunt might be tried. He trotted forward until he stood on the grass.

The pitch. The batter turned to bunt, and David charged in. It was a slow grounder just inside the third-base line. David ran as hard as he could. He fielded the ball with both hands, pivoted on his right foot and whipped the ball underhand to first.

A good throw! It was close!

"Safe!" cried the umpire.

David spun, saw that Bonesy was covering third, then took his time walking back. He played on the grass again. It was still a bunt situation.

Again the Canaries bunted! This time the ball was hit too hard. David fielded it. He pegged to second. Out by a step!

Jimmy didn't try the play to first.

"Nice play, David!" shouted Bonesy.

One out. Men on first and third.

A pop fly over Rex's head. He caught it for the second out.

The fans of both teams were shouting wildly now. The Flickers' infielders were chattering like monkeys. It was a way to keep from thinking in these tense, anxious moments.

Crack! A hard grounder to David's right side! He turned, then lunged after it for a back-handed catch. The ball brushed the tip of his glove and bounded to the outfield. A run scored. The hitter went to second.

Now there were runners on second and third.

Coach Beach called time. He left the dugout and talked a bit with Brad. David thought he would put in another pitcher, but he didn't. The next batter popped up to first, and the sides retired.

Score: Canaries 5; Flickers 3.

"Hold them, Canaries!" shouted the Canaries' fans. "Strike them out, Rocky!"

Rex led off. He waited Rocky out and won a free ticket to first. Perhaps Rocky was afraid to pitch him anything good.

Marty waited till Rocky put a strike over the plate, then belted a single over Rocky's head. Bonesy socked a grounder to short. The shortstop fielded the ball nicely, fired it to second and got Marty out. The second baseman whipped the ball to first. Bonesy, running as fast as his legs could go, made it by half a step.

The Canaries booed the umpire, and for a moment the first baseman said a thing or two to him. The umpire said a thing or two back, and the first baseman shied away.

Coach Beach chuckled. "Never underestimate the power of an umpire," he said.

David pressed the helmet down comfortably on his head and waited for Rocky to pitch. He had made up his mind to swing at the first good one that came in.

Rocky toed the rubber, looked at the runners on base, then delivered. It was high.

Rocky came in with the next pitch, and David swung. His bat met the ball solidly, and he knew instantly that this time the ball was going.

He saw the first-base coach smiling and swinging his arm like a windmill, urging David on to second. David kept going. He saw that the ball

had just struck the fence in left center field, that it had bounced back and both left and center fielders were chasing after it.

He rounded second and went on to third. He reached the base standing up for the longest triple he had ever hit, scoring Rex and Bonesy.

Steve Pierce belted his second single of the game, scoring David. The coach had Jerry Hines pinch-hit for Brad. Jerry flied out, then Ken struck out to end the big inning.

"Beautiful hit, David," said the coach. "Too bad it wasn't just a wee bit higher."

David grinned. "Thanks," he said. He turned and went out to the field.

The Flickers were ahead now, 6 to 5. David felt good. Now, if only the Flickers could protect that lead.

The Canaries didn't get a man past first base that bottom half of the fifth. In the top of the sixth Herm Simmons pinch-hit for Chugger. He singled to start things off for the Flickers. Jimmy laid down a sacrifice bunt, putting Herm on second. Rex lifted a long fly to center that was caught.

Marty drilled a liner at the third baseman. The third sacker fumbled it and was puzzled for a moment trying to find it. He finally picked it up just a few feet behind him. The second-base coach had Herm play it safe.

It turned out to be a good idea, for Bonesy blasted out a double and Herm scored. David fouled two pitches, then struck out.

The Canaries were solemn birds as they came to bat for the last time. Even their fans had become saddened and quiet.

Jerry, pitching now in place of Brad, walked the first batter. There followed two outs in succession. Then the Canaries began belting the ball. They scored a run and had two men on bases when David fielded a ground ball and touched third for the last out.

The Flickers jumped and yelled with joy at the victory. They had played the best team in the league and had won. They had clipped the Canaries' wings.

Ann Marie smiled proudly at David as they left the ballpark and headed for home. "That was a beautiful hit, David," she said. "You played wonderfully today."

"Sure did," said Dad. "I wish Don could have been here to see you."

David smiled. He had bobbled a couple today, but that triple with two men on bases had sure made things a lot brighter.

11

DAD took David with him to the hospital later that evening to bring Don home. Don was glad to leave — but not especially so. As a nurse pushed Don out of his room and down the long white corridor, other nurses looked on regretfully.

David grinned. Don's magnetic personality had even conquered the nurses.

Dad helped Don onto the backseat of the car, then placed the two crutches in beside him. Don thanked the nurse, said good-bye to her and leaned back comfortably against the seat.

"Home, Dad," he said.

He sat with his bad leg on the seat. David, sitting beside Dad, saw that the cast was covered with autographs. Probably every visitor from school had signed his or her name on it.

After they drove awhile Don asked David about how the Flickers were doing. And how he was doing at third.

"We beat the Canaries today," replied David. "I had two errors," he added solemnly.

"But he hit a triple and knocked in two runs," said Dad. "He helped win the ball game."

Don's face brightened. "Fine," he said. "Wait'll tomorrow. We'll go down to the field and give you a workout. Third base is a lot tougher than a lot of people think."

"You're telling me," said David. It took a player like Don to realize a thing like that.

There was much rejoicing when Don got home. Mom and Ann Marie kissed him, and Ann Marie immediately began telling him about a dozen things that had happened in and around town, hardly giving Mom a chance to squeeze in a word. Dad laughed. David shook his head in puzzlement. Where had he ever got such a talkative sister? Don just sat there, smiling happily about the whole thing. You could see that he was certainly pleased to be home.

The following morning David telephoned Bonesy to tell him that he and Don were going to the ballpark. Would Bonesy like to come along? Bonesy would.

On their way to the park — Ann Marie went, too — they met Rex Drake and Marty Cass. The boys were glad to see Don and were willing to practice with them. They looked at Ann Marie and the glove on her hand with suspicion, though, then rushed home after their gloves.

Under Don's direction, Bonesy hit grounders to David at third. Ann Marie backed up her brother. She picked up and threw in the grounders that David missed. She had played pitch and catch with David for several years and could throw well.

After they had worked out awhile a car drove into the parking lot and stopped. Two people walked in through the gate. David recognized them immediately. Mr. and Mrs. Finch! What were they doing here?

They walked up to Don, smiled and shook his hand. David heard them ask Don about his leg. Then he heard Mrs. Finch say, "You just won't give up, will you?"

Don laughed. "I guess not, Mrs. Finch," he said.

"And you want your brother to be a baseball player like yourself?"

"No," said Don. "I want him to be better than I am."

Mrs. Finch shook her head. "I can't understand it," she said. "You boys spending your precious time out here hitting a little white ball all over the place and then chasing it just so it can be hit all over again. Really now, Don, is that practical? Does it make sense?"

Don shrugged. "There are millions of Americans who think so, Mrs. Finch. And, I bet, so does Mr. Finch."

Mr. Finch, a big man with graying hair, grunted. "I never played baseball, Don. Football was my sport. But I'm a fan, I'll tell you that."

"Never mind asking Mr. Finch," said Mrs. Finch. "Sometimes I think he's still a boy."

Mr. Finch grunted again, and Don laughed.

"Why don't you come to a game, Mrs. Finch?" invited Don. "These boys play tomorrow. Why don't you come with Mr. Finch? You will understand better maybe watching it why kids just never grow up when it comes to playing baseball."

Mrs. Finch looked hard at Don. "I doubt that, Don," she said. "But to show you that I'm not bullheaded, I will have Mr. Finch bring me."

The Finches left, and the boys broke out in laughter.

"Bet she won't be there," said Rex.

"Oh, yes, she will," said David. "You don't know Mrs. Finch!"

That evening the *Penwood Times* carried a short article in the sports section about the Flickers-Canaries game.

Big guns for the Flickers were Marty Cass and Bonesy Lane with four and three hits respectively. David Kroft, the Flickers' third baseman, smashed out a triple against the left center field fence that brought in two runs. Then he scored on a single by Steve Pierce.

It was a great victory for the Flickers. This was the first game the Canaries had lost out of eight.

The box score:

	AB	H	RBI	R
Lacey 2b	4	1	0	1
Hines rf	3	2	0	1
dSimmons rf	1	1	0	1
Merrill 1b	4	0	0	0
Drake c	2	1	0	2
Cass lf	4	4	2	0
Lane ss	4	3	2	1

Mulligan 3b	1	0	0	0
[a]Kroft 3b	3	1	2	1
Hill cf	1	0	0	0
[b]Pierce cf	2	2	1	0
Lodge p	2	1	0	0
[c]Hines p	1	0	0	0
Totals	32	16	7	7

a — Flied out for Mulligan in 4th; b — Singled for Hill in 4th; c — Flied out for Lodge in 5th; d — Singled for Hines in 6th.

Flickers	. . .	0 1 2 0 3 1 — 7
Canaries	. . .	2 1 1 1 0 1 — 6

12

THE weather was chilly Friday morning, the day the Flickers were to play the Bluebirds. By noon it was warmer. But the sky remained gray and overcast. David hoped it would not rain.

It didn't.

Again the game started with him on the bench and Legs on third base. David wondered what Don would think. Don was sitting in the stands with Ann Marie, Mom and Dad.

Jerry was on the mound for the Flickers. He had trouble getting the ball over the plate that first inning. His southpaw deliveries were mostly outside. He walked two men before he found the plate. Then the Bluebirds began to hit the ball, and two runs scored before the Flickers could get them out.

The Flickers evened the score, though, with a walk by Ken, a single by Jimmy and a double off the bat of Rex Drake.

Legs, leading off in the second inning, struck out. But then another hitting spree started, and the Flickers chalked up three more runs.

The Bluebirds scored once at their turn at bat, then held the Flickers from getting a runner past first. The first two outs were on a double play by the shortstop. He snared Bonesy's line drive and threw out Marty Cass at first before Marty could tag up on the play. Then Legs grounded out to second.

The Bluebirds kept hitting and scoring, but so did the Flickers. It was a ball game with lots of noise from the people in the grandstand.

Suddenly David heard a voice that was kind

of familiar, although he was sure he had never heard it at the ball park before.

"Come on, Jerry! Hit that ball! Sock it over the fence!"

The voice was coming from someone behind the dugout. It was a loud voice. And it was a woman's.

David smiled. He knew who that woman was.

Jerry didn't sock one over the fence. But later on Rex Drake did with two men on bases. When it was Legs Mulligan's turn at bat, Coach Beach had David pinch-hit for him. David blasted a double. But he died on second as Windy Hill flied out to center.

The Bluebirds hit two to David that inning as if they had hoped he would get into the game to help them out. David missed the first one, a hot grounder to his left side.

"Come on, David!" yelled a fan. "A Kroft isn't supposed to miss an easy grounder like that!"

David blushed.

The second was a high bouncing ball, which he caught. Quickly he pegged the ball to second, forcing out the runner. Second baseman Jimmy Merrill whipped the ball to first, and the hitter was out on a nice double play.

"Now you're looking like a Kroft!" cried the same voice.

"Thataboy, David!" yelled another voice. "Fine play!"

That was Mrs. Finch. She caught his eye and waved to him. He smiled and waved back. It was almost impossible to believe that she was sitting there in the stands, yelling as if she were a regular baseball fan. Beside her was Mr. Finch. He was looking at her and grinning, too.

Just behind them sat Ann Marie, Don, Dad and Mom. All four of them were laughing heartily over the way Mrs. Finch shouted and jumped excitedly on the seat.

Dad said something to Mrs. Finch, and she turned and looked around at him. Then she looked away from Dad and didn't make a peep

for almost half an inning. Afterward she started in yelling again, and for the rest of the game Dad didn't say any more to her.

Maybe, thought David, she was going to like baseball after all. And Dad certainly would not want to discourage her.

The Flickers led 10 to 7 going into the sixth inning. The Bluebirds put one run across, but that was all. The Flickers won it 10 to 8.

David saw Dad and the rest of the family walking out of the ballpark with Mr. and Mrs. Finch. Everyone was laughing except Mrs. Finch. Which was natural.

At home David said, "Do you think Mrs. Finch has changed her mind about baseball, Dad? She sure did a lot of hollering at the game."

Dad smiled. "She didn't want to admit it when I asked her that same question," replied Dad. "However, I think her crust isn't as hard as she pretends it is."

Dad bowled at eight o'clock. Usually, David and Ann Marie went with him on Friday nights. Tonight, Ann Marie stayed home, and David and Don went.

"Well," said Dad as he started to sit down to put on his bowling shoes, "look in Lane Number Four. Am I seeing things, or is that really *her*?"

The boys stared.

Bowling in Lane Number Four was Mrs. Finch! Of course Mr. Finch was bowling, too. But everyone in Penwood knew that Mr. Finch bowled.

"Just a minute," said Dad. He went over to the Finches and watched Mrs. Finch throw the big black ball down the lane. The ball knocked down three pins. Mrs. Finch snapped her fingers disgustedly, turned around and stopped. She was staring at Dad.

"Mr. Kroft," she said, "are you spying on me?"

Dad laughed. "This is my bowling night, too,"

he said. Then he added, "Mrs. Finch, is it possible that you're becoming soft? That you really don't think sports are so bad after all?"

Mrs. Finch glared at him. "I won't answer that question," she said, "on the grounds that it might incriminate me."

She turned to David and Don, her eyes snapping. "Your father," she said, "just loves to argue!"

The boys burst out laughing. They knew that Mrs. Finch was really having a wonderful time.

13

IN the next two games David showed improvement at third base. He even passed Bonesy in a one-hundred-yard sprint. He knew he would never be as good a ballpayer as Dad, or Don, or any of the other Kroft boys, though.

He was a fair hitter. After that last game his batting average was .289. But even Don hinted that David wasn't doing as well as he should at the hot corner.

"Sometimes you're playing the ball as if you're depending a lot on the shortstop," said Don. "You can't do that. You must go after every ball you can."

On Sunday afternoon — the first Sunday of August — David and Bonesy went bike riding in the country. It was a lovely day, and they hadn't taken a long trip on their bikes in weeks.

The sun was bright and hot. As the boys pedaled along the road, the trees on the distant hills looked purple and blue. A field of buttercups sparkled like a sea of yellow dust.

They arrived at a picnic area, rested, then rode on.

At last they reached a small village. They bought a bottle of Coke each to quench their thirsts, then got on their bikes and started back for home.

They took their time. They were not in a hurry. They talked about baseball — about their own team and also the major leagues. They talked about David's coin collection and about Mrs. Finch. They talked about Don's bad leg and whether he would ever be as good a ballplayer as before. They talked about a lot of things.

Before they realized it, they were back in Penwood. And the long ride had made them hungry.

They rode up the sidewalk, Bonesy riding behind David. Finally, Bonesy turned up the street on which he lived.

"See you later, David," he said.

"Okay," said David.

It had been a long, pleasant ride. And it seemed to have ended so quickly.

David rode on.

A dog began to bark behind him. David looked back and recognized a new dog in the neighborhood. It belonged to the Elwoods.

Let him bark, thought David.

Soon he reached the corner where the Finches' big white house stood.

Just as he started to turn the corner, the dog ran up beside him. His bark turned into a growl, and he lunged at David's leg.

David swerved so quickly that he lost control of the bike. The bike swerved into the Finches'

111

yard and struck the statue of a boy holding up
a sign with THE FINCHES printed on it.

The statue fell over and struck the sidewalk
leading up to the Finches' front porch.

It crashed into many pieces.

14

DAVID looked in dismay at the pieces and then at the Finches' house. There was no one on the porch. No one looking from a window.

He turned around. The dog that had caused him to run into the statue was trotting down the sidewalk, returning home quietly as if he were satisfied with the job he had done.

David yanked out the kickstand of his bike and parked it on the walk. He went up to the house, trembling all the way. He knocked on the door.

There was no answer. He knocked again. Still no answer.

He went back to his bike, took it home and told Mom what he had done.

"It was an accident," said Mom. "Don't feel so badly about it. Just tell Mrs. Finch exactly what happened."

"But what about the statue?" asked David. "I'll probably have to pay for that."

Mom nodded. "I'm afraid somebody will have to pay for it," she said.

"I'd better put the pieces in a box," said David.

Just after noontime Mr. and Mrs. Finch came home in their car. David saw them get out and go look at the box on the walk and what was left of the broken statue. He saw the expressions on their faces. And he had a good idea of what Mrs. Finch must be saying.

A little while later he went over there. He knocked on the door. Mrs. Finch answered it.

"Why, hello, David," she greeted him pleasantly. "Come in."

He stepped into the house. He was trembling again, more than before.

"Mrs. Finch," he said, "that statue out there. I broke it with my bike. A dog chased me, and I ran into it."

"Oh," she said. "Mr. Finch and I wondered what could have happened."

David held out the paper sack he held in his hand. "That statue must have cost a lot of money, Mrs. Finch," he said. "I wouldn't want to ask my dad to pay for it. I'll pay for it with my own money."

"What is this, David?" asked Mrs. Finch as she took the paper sack from him.

"It's my quarter coin collection. There are some missing, but I think there are enough there to pay for the statue. If there aren't —"
He paused.

Mrs. Finch had the folder open, looking at

116

the coins. She didn't say anything for a long while. Then she cleared her throat and smiled.

"No, David," she said. "I can't accept this. This is something special. Something you have worked a long time for."

"That's all right, Mrs. Finch," said David. "I have a dime collection, too. And I can start in with quarters any time. Please take them."

Mrs. Finch smiled. "Okay, David. If you insist. Thank you very much. And thank you for coming over and telling me about it. If you hadn't, we — well, we probably would never have found out."

David left the house. His heart was heavy. He had spent a long, long time collecting those coins.

15

THE next day, Monday, the Flickers played the Canaries. There was one more game — on Wednesday — and the season would be over.

The Canaries had the league pretty well sewed up. They had nine wins and only one loss. The Flickers had seven wins and three losses. The Flickers were in second place.

Coach Beach started David at third. He had moved him up in the lineup, too. David was to bat fifth, right after Rex Drake.

The game started, and for the first two innings David didn't get a ball at third. He wished he would. He felt sure he could catch almost any grounder that came to him. Playing nearly all summer and practicing almost every day made him feel that way.

In the third he got one. A hard grounder that was hit straight at him. He caught the hop, pegged to first, and the runner was out.

Then, with two on, a ground ball was hit to him again. This one he fumbled! By the time he picked it up it was too late.

He looked around quickly. The two runners on bases had not dared to advance. The bases were now loaded.

Mandy Rubens, the Canaries' slugger, pounded out a single. Two runs scored. That was all the Canaries got that inning. But it was enough to put them one ahead of the Flickers.

David had more chances at third and handled them without a bobble. Coach Beach made substitutions but, much to David's surprise, left David in the game.

The Flickers tied it up in the fifth, 7 to 7.

The Flickers' fans began to yell louder than ever. David could not mistake one of the voices especially. Mrs. Finch's.

Nobody would have believed it — but it was true. She had become a baseball fan.

The Flickers were up in the bottom of the sixth and won it when Rex pounded out a long triple with Jimmy Merrill on first base. It was a glorious victory.

Score: Flickers 8; Canaries 7.

"Played fine out there, brother, boy," Don said as they walked out of the ballpark.

David wasn't too pleased.

"That error I made cost us two runs," he said. "That wasn't good."

"But a lot of balls came to you after that, and you caught them," said Don. "And you got two hits. That's very good, brother."

The coach started David again in the Bluebirds game on Wednesday. The Bluebirds had had a very poor season. They had won only one game so far and lost nine.

121

Southpaw Jerry Hines pitched against them and had difficulty from the very first inning.

When he walked a man, the next hitter would bunt. David certainly had a workout at third during those early innings. Jerry fielded one bunt, which was laid down between the pitcher's box and first base. But the others were directed to third.

The bunts helped the Bluebirds. The score was tied 2 and 2 going into the top of the fifth inning. This was a surprise to the Flickers' fans. They had expected the game to be a runaway for their team.

Rex, leading off, smashed out a double. David followed it up with another double, scoring Rex. Marty Cass got on when the second baseman missed a pop fly. The Flickers' fans cheered lustily. It looked as if this was going to be the Flickers' big inning.

Then things began to go wrong for the Flickers. Bonesy tried to bunt to advance the runners. His bunt turned out to be a blooping fly ball to the pitcher. The pitcher caught it and whipped it to first before Marty could get back. Windy grounded out, and that was it.

The Bluebirds' leadoff man doubled to start things well for them. The next hitter drove a hard sizzling grounder to third, just inside the bag. David dove after it. The ball struck his glove and glanced off into foul territory. He got up, raced after it and picked it up. He saw the runner bolting for home and pegged the ball.

It zipped through the air straight as a string for Rex's mitt. The Bluebirds' player hit the dirt just as Rex caught the ball and put it on him.

"Out!" cried the umpire.

The Flickers' fans went wild.

"Thataway to throw that ball, David boy!"

"Nice stop, David!"

He could hear Don and Dad and Ann Marie and Mom. And amid all those shouts he heard Mrs. Finch, too.

In the sixth the Flickers picked up another run to make it 4 to 2. The Bluebirds put one across at their time at bat, but that was all they could do. They lost to the Flickers, 4 to 3, in a game that was thrilling to the very last out.

"Beautiful play you made there on third, David," said Don, as he hobbled on his crutches alongside his brother.

"Thanks. But I'll never be a real good ball-player," said David. "Never as good as you. Nor Dad. Nor any of our uncles."

"You have time," said Don. "You're still young, brother."

Dad put an arm around David's shoulders. "Don't worry about being real good, son," he said. "You did the best you can, and that's all anyone expects."

"You should have heard Mrs. Finch yelling," chimed in Ann Marie. "She sure rooted for you, David!"

"I sure did," said a voice behind them.

They looked around, and there was Mrs. Finch herself, and Mr. Finch. "You played a fine game, David."

"Thanks." David grinned.

"By the way, I'd like to have you stop at our house before you go home. Can you do that?"

Uh-oh! She has another job for Bonesy and me, thought David. Well, baseball season was all over with. It would make no difference how late they were now.

"I think so," he said. He looked at Mom and Dad. They smiled and nodded. It was all right with them.

"How about riding back with us?" suggested Mr. Finch.

David smiled. "Okay."

They arrived at the house. Mrs. Finch asked David to sit down. He sat there, his cap in his hand, while Mrs. Finch stepped out of the room. Mr. Finch talked to him about the game a bit, then Mrs. Finch returned. She was holding a paper sack in her hand.

David stared at the sack. It was flat. It looked very familiar.

"Here, David," she said. "I'm returning your

coins to you. I've decided that a boy who gives up his wonderful coin collection to pay for a small statue is made of good, honest stuff. I'd rather know that you're that kind of boy than the greatest player in all Penwood."

David stared at Mrs. Finch. And he had thought that she was going to give him another job!

"Thanks, Mrs. Finch," he said, happily. "Thanks a lot!"

He started for the door.

"Don't you want to check it?" asked Mrs. Finch. "See if I didn't lose any of it while I had it?"

David pulled the folder out of the sack and opened it. His eyes bulged. Other than the empty slots for coins to be minted the next year and the next, all the slots were filled! Mrs. Finch had gotten the missing coins herself and had brought the folder up to date!

David swallowed. "Mrs. Finch, I — I think you're great! Real great! And any time you want

Bonesy and me to clean up your yard — or do anything — just let us know!"

Mrs. Finch's hands were clasped tightly together in front of her. She smiled and blinked her eyes several times before she spoke again.

"Tell your dad and mother," she said, "that Mr. Finch and I would like to bowl with them sometime."

David grinned. "I sure will!" he said.

He put the folder back into the sack and went out the door.

He ran down the walk, then paused a moment. There, in the same spot the statue had been before it was broken, was a brand-new one. This was the first time he had seen it.

It was a statue of a boy sitting on a stone and holding out the same sign: THE FINCHES. The boy was smiling.

And he was wearing a baseball cap.

How many of these Matt Christopher sports classics have you read?

- ❏ Baseball Pals
- ❏ The Basket Counts
- ❏ Catch That Pass!
- ❏ Catcher with a Glass Arm
- ❏ Challenge at Second Base
- ❏ The Counterfeit Tackle
- ❏ The Diamond Champs
- ❏ Dirt Bike Racer
- ❏ Dirt Bike Runaway
- ❏ Face-Off
- ❏ Football Fugitive
- ❏ The Fox Steals Home
- ❏ The Great Quarterback Switch
- ❏ Hard Drive to Short
- ❏ The Hockey Machine
- ❏ Ice Magic
- ❏ Johnny Long Legs
- ❏ The Kid Who Only Hit Homers
- ❏ Little Lefty
- ❏ Long Shot for Paul
- ❏ Long Stretch at First Base
- ❏ Look Who's Playing First Base
- ❏ Miracle at the Plate
- ❏ No Arm in Left Field
- ❏ Red-Hot Hightops
- ❏ Run, Billy, Run
- ❏ Shortstop from Tokyo
- ❏ Soccer Halfback
- ❏ The Submarine Pitch
- ❏ Tackle Without a Team
- ❏ Tight End
- ❏ Too Hot to Handle
- ❏ Touchdown for Tommy
- ❏ Tough to Tackle
- ❏ Wingman on Ice
- ❏ The Year Mom Won the Pennant

All available in paperback from Little, Brown and Company